Date Due

MAY 2 6 1995

MAY 0 8 REC'D

DEC 0 8 2003

DEC 0 4 REC'D

OCT 2 7 2004

OCT 2 7 REC'D

FEB 1 4 REC'D

THE ANIMAL HOUSE

Ivor Cutler &
Helen Oxenbury

William Morrow and Company
New York 1977

Published in the United States in 1977.

Text copyright © 1976 by Ivor Cutler
Illustrations copyright © 1976 by Helen Oxenbury

Published in Great Britain in 1976.

1 2 3 4 5 6 7 8 9 10

Library of Congress Cataloging in Publication Data

Cutler, Ivor.
    The animal house.

    SUMMARY: The Diamond family finds temporary shelter
in a house built by their friends from the zoo.
    [1. Dwellings—Fiction. 2. Animals—Fiction.
3. Zoo animals—Fiction]
I. Oxenbury, Helen. II. Title.
PZ7.C978An   [E]   77-4468
ISBN 0-688-22110-6
ISBN 0-688-32110-0 lib. bdg.

One morning Simon Diamond woke up.
He found the house gone.

"I *thought* it was windy last night,"
said his mother, as they bent over their eggs
and shivered below the morning sun.

"I'll do something," muttered his dad,
fastening on an old cloak.

When Mr. Diamond reached the zoo, he asked his
mates if they had seen the house.

"I saw it plump into the sea, Mr. D.," rumbled Mr.
Softwater, the head keeper.

"In that case, I'll need a new one!" Diamond sighed
and dipped a morning coffee biscuit lazily into his tea.

"You know there are no empty houses around here," whispered Mr. Cello, the lion keeper, who had a sore throat from doing imitations.

Mr. Diamond raised his head. "Are you in a good mood, Benjamin?" he inquired.

The head keeper grinned and flashed his teeth. "You know me. It's my only mood."

Dennis Diamond smiled back. "Then can I borrow some animals to make a temporary dwelling? Not many."

Benjamin Softwater pulled out his notebook and sketched. The keepers watched, fascinated.

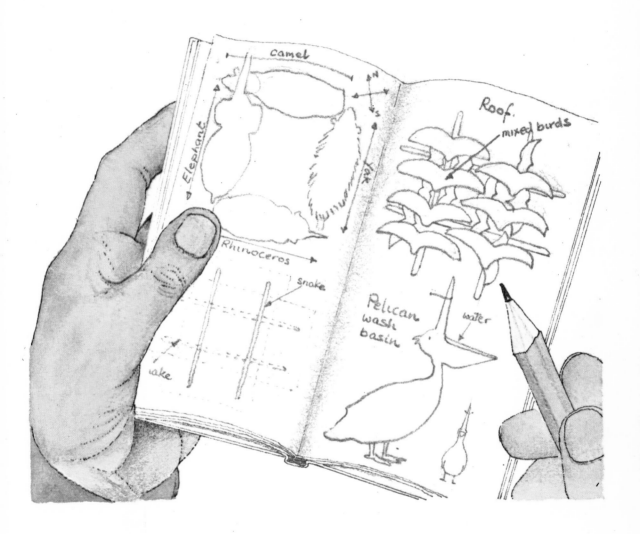

"Now, Mr. Diamond, if you took an elephant, a camel, a rhinoceros, and a yak, you'd have your walls. Then a few long snakes for perches, and some mixed birds with large wings to perch on them. And, let's see, a pelican's beak to wash your hands and face in. That do it?"

Dennis Diamond turned to the head keeper, threw his arms around him, and kissed his nose by mistake. "You're such a nice man!" he choked, tears pouring out of his eyes.

Benjamin Softwater's face went dark beetroot with embarrassment. "Dennis Diamond, you do that again and you're fired. Collect your creatures when it's time to go home." And he strolled away, followed by the loving glances of his assistants.

What a lovely man, they thought, and went off to clean the cages.

Simon's eyes popped out at six o'clock
when the creatures arrived.

The elephant faced the yak.
The rhinoceros faced the camel.
All together they made a square.

"Lie stiff!" ordered Mr. Diamond, and laid the boa constrictors across the elephant and rhinoceros.

Instantly a small cloud of eagles, keas, condors, emus, and a vulture rose and roosted on them with spread wings—a warm, watertight roof.

The pelican sat on the elephant's toes.

Hundreds of fireflies flew and pulsed inside the new
house. The family held their breath. It was fairyland.

Mrs. Diamond cooked supper
over a jar of the tiny gleaming sparks.

At nightfall, the animals lay on their sides, legs out. Mrs. Diamond snuggled deep into yak fur, and Mr. Diamond, who liked a hard pillow, lay back against the rhino. It felt crusty and warm, like newly baked bread.

The camel's woolly humps seemed to Simon the most exciting bed in the world. He lay between them gazing up at the fireflies till he fell asleep.

"What happened?" asked Simon
the following day, as he shivered in
the morning sun and bent over his eggs.

"They wandered away." Artificial
Diamond, his mum, sighed. "Daddy's
looking for them."

Dennis Diamond shuffled into the zoo,
head bent, and bumped into Benjamin
Softwater. He looked up. Benjamin was
smiling gently, and his gray eyes twinkled.

"Benjamin—" started Dennis, in a small voice.

Benjamin held himself and roared with
laughter. "My animals have returned!" he
gasped finally. "Now go down to the seashore.
There's something there for you."

I wonder what it is, thought Dennis, as he walked
along the sandy road, feeling more cheerful.

Floating on the sea, bumping gently
against the rocks, was his house.

Climbing onto the verandah, he entered the front door. The house was just as it had left him, except where a sharp rock had torn a diamond-shaped hole in Simon's floor.

Dennis lay on Simon's bed to think. Gradually he realized that he was enjoying the quiet movement and the soft bumping.

"Why not?" he shouted, and jumped up. He pulled
the clothesline out of the cupboard, tied the house to a
rock, and went for his family.

They were delighted to live on the sea. Dennis fixed
a pane of strong glass over the hole in Simon's floor so
that Simon could enjoy the fish at night with his flashlight.

Dennis brought hundreds of spare fireflies
from the zoo and filled the house with them.

Mrs. Diamond bought a machine
that turned seawater into drinking water.

Every Sunday evening the keepers visit the Diamonds, sit on the back verandah drinking lemonade made from real lemons with water out of Artificial's machine, and gaze at the sun setting into the sea.

"The wind blew you into happiness." Mr. Softwater smiles, and everyone sits, quiet, feeling the house move about underneath them, waiting for the soft, little bumps.